The Story of Alexander the Great

The Story of
Alexander the Great

Sofia Zarabouka

The J. Paul Getty Museum   Los Angeles

PROLOGUE

In 356 b.c. Alexander the Great, son of King Philip, was born in the northern Greek city of Aiges in Macedonia. At that time the mainland and islands of Greece were divided into small states. Greek city-states also spread from the Black Sea to every shore of the Mediterranean.

Each state had its own leader, and although they all spoke the same language and considered themselves Greeks, it was not uncommon for them to fight among themselves. King Philip proved to be the strongest of the leaders and set about organizing all the Greeks against the Persians.

In the spring of 336 b.c., the sudden death of Philip brought Alexander to the Macedonian throne. At the age of only twenty, Alexander the Great found himself the leader of 30,000 foot soldiers and 5,000 cavalry. He was exceptionally brave and well educated and had a passion for advancing the Greek nation. Immediately he went ahead with a great expedition against the king of Persia, Darius. In a series of battles, the Persians were defeated. After the death of Darius, Alexander was expected to return to Greece. But apart from being a conqueror, he also had a strong sense of adventure and decided to continue eastward through present-day Turkey into Syria, Egypt, Iraq, Iran, Afghanistan, Pakistan, and, finally, India, before heading back west. Along the way he founded cities that bore his name, Alexandria in Egypt being the most famous.

In the spring of 323 B.C., at the age of almost thirty-three, Alexander died of fever in the city of Babylon. It had taken him only a little more than ten years to create an empire of a million and a half square miles. He himself had covered 25,000 miles over three continents. He was one of the greatest generals of all time, a brilliant tactician who never lost a battle, and an excellent student of human character. He explored far beyond the geographical boundaries known at that time and discovered new territories. He charted new trade routes and made Greek the common language in the areas he conquered. Last but not least: in changing the world, he changed himself with it.

THE STORY OF ALEXANDER THE GREAT

According to Greek tradition, in the course of great storms, when the sky is full of dark clouds and the waves grow as high as mountains, a mermaid springs out of the waters, seizes the first ship she encounters, and makes it stop.

"Is King Alexander alive and well?" she asks in a fierce tone of voice. Then the person facing her must find the courage to answer: "He's alive and well and he rules the world!"

At once the waters become calm and the mermaid, who happens to be the favorite sister of Alexander the Great, allows the ship to continue its voyage. Whoever dares to tell her the truth—namely, that Alexander the Great has been dead for over 2,000 years—cannot escape her wrath. The mermaid lifts the boat and dashes it deep into the dark waters. The sea swallows it up and it is lost for ever.

There are many stories about Alexander. Some are real and others are legend. In actual fact, many centuries have passed since his death; and yet, unlike other conquerors, people still remember him. So there must have been something good and worth loving in him, because otherwise they would not go on talking about him.

He is remembered not only in Greece, where he was born, but also in all the places where he ruled, perhaps because he respected the people he conquered and wanted to learn their customs. In some cases, he even emulated them. He dressed the way they did, tasted the food they ate, participated in their festive celebrations, and listened attentively to their viewpoints.

He tried to understand their way of life instead of forcing his own lifestyle on them. This is why the stories and legends of all the peoples he conquered present him in local dress and familiar with customs totally unknown in his birthplace.

A few years ago in Vergina, which is an ancient site near the city of Salonika, archaeologists discovered the tomb of Alexander's father, Philip. On a mound near the ruins of an old palace, they excavated carefully until they uncovered a royal tomb. It had been there all these centuries, although no one knew anything about it.

A gold chest was found containing Philip's bones wrapped in a piece of purple material and crowned by a gold wreath. Nearby, the archaeologists also discovered the king's armor, along with various personal objects. Thus we know that King Philip lived and died in Macedonia.

Alexander the Great, son of Philip, was born there too. His mother was the daughter of the king of the neighboring city-state of Epiros, and her name was Olympias. The young prince was not allowed any pampering by his parents. They did not want to spoil him, so they demanded that his teachers be strict. Most of his time was devoted to exercising and learning the use of weapons. Young Alexander was fearless.

There is a story about a black stallion that one day started running wildly through the courtyard. Five trainers chased it but were unable to mount it. All of a sudden the horse stopped short. Not a soul dared to approach except young Alexander, who moved swiftly, mounting and mastering the steed. Henceforth the proud horse belonged to Alexander and was called Bucephalos, which means "The One with the Head of an Ox."

When Alexander became a teenager, his father asked the famous philosopher Aristotle to tutor the prince in politics, philosophy, poetry, and drama.

Throughout Philip's reign the Persians were the main enemy of the Greek city-states. While the Greeks were at war among themselves, the Persians were busy defeating the Greek cities in Asia Minor—present-day Turkey. The Athenians, who were the traditional leaders of the other city-states, did not approve of Philip's growing power in the north. So they decided to fight him at Chaironeia, not too far from the city-state of Thebes, a neighbor of Athens.

Alexander took part in that battle, displaying great courage. The Athenians suffered a bitter loss. Most of their men were killed. Alexander's father demanded that the young prince escort the ashes of the dead Athenians back to their city to be buried there. Alexander was delighted to agree, because he was an admirer of Athenian culture.

After this battle Philip was accepted by everybody as commander-in-chief of the Greeks against the Persian threat, except by the Spartans in the peninsula of Peloponnesos. Each city-state was free and independent but was required to supply Philip with soldiers and weapons.

By the summer of 336 B.C., everything was ready for an expedition to Asia. Before his departure, Philip organized games and festivities to celebrate his daughter's marriage. Accompanied by his court, he entered the theater to attend a performance given especially for the occasion. Suddenly a young man rushed upon him out of the crowd and stabbed him to death. That was the end of Philip.

At the tender age of twenty, Alexander was obliged to take his father's place. His first act was to gather around him all his childhood friends: Hephaistion, Krateros, Seleucus, Ptolemy, and Perdiccas. These men took charge of the infantry and cavalry under King and General Alexander.

And so the expedition to Asia began. In addition to the Macedonian army, Alexander was in command of 7,000 foot soldiers from various city-states and 1,800 horsemen from the city-state of Thessaly.

There were also the camp followers, women, servants, and craftsmen. His entourage also included botanists, geographers, and even historians, who recorded the details of how the expedition was progressing.

After crossing the Hellespont, the waterway between Europe and Asia, Alexander reached the shores of Asia Minor. When he set foot on land, he seized a spear and stuck it in the ground.

"This land is ours!" he exclaimed.

King Darius of Persia, who was known as the King of Kings and whose kingdom was truly vast, paid no attention at all to this bold young man. Confident of his own power, he let Alexander advance.

Darius's empire spread all the way from Egypt to the Indus River and comprised deserts, mountains, fertile valleys, and big rivers. Many different peoples lived under Persian rule. They were free to speak their own languages and worship their own gods. But each tribe was governed by one of the noble Persian families devoted to Darius. However, his army was not at all in good shape. Many of his soldiers had become used to a luxurious way of life and had become lazy and lackadaisical.

Alexander, on the contrary, was full of vim and vigor. He believed his ancestors went back to Achilles, the Greek hero, and to the Greek demigod Herakles. Alexander was reared on the heroic stories of adventures told in the *Iliad* and the *Odyssey*. That is why the very first thing he did in Asia Minor was to visit Troy, a coastal city where in earlier times the heroic war adventures of the *Iliad* took place. When he found Achilles' grave there, he placed a wreath upon it.

In May 334 B.C., the Persian generals decided that Alexander was going too far and should be taught a lesson. So they gathered their cavalry and infantry along the banks of the Granikos River. There were millions of them. But Alexander was quite undaunted and led his men into battle, spreading panic in the hearts of the Persians. He was present on all fronts, astride his black steed, Bucephalos.

At many points his life was in danger, since everyone had their eyes on him and he was the target of every general of the enemy. But Alexander remained unharmed, and, finally, the Persians were forced to beat a hasty retreat.

Following his victory, Alexander marched on south to Sardis, a flourishing city of Asia Minor. There he acted cleverly. Instead of dismissing the local rulers, he let them stay on and keep their privileges. At the same time he appointed a Greek overseer. Thus his enemies had no choice but to collaborate with him.

After taking the coastal cities of Ephesos and Halikarnassos— summer was over now—Alexander decided to spend the winter in Gordion in the heart of Asia Minor. As soon as he arrived there, he was told the prophecy of the Gordian knot. According to an oracle, whoever managed to untie the intricate knot on the pole of a particular chariot was destined to become master of Asia.

Alexander asked to be taken to the chariot at once. But when he saw the knot, he realized that it was impossible to undo. So he wielded his sword with an energetic thrust and cut the knot in two. "There now!" he said, "I have undone the Gordian knot!"

With the spring of 333 B.C., the armies of Alexander moved on again until they reached the renowned Persian port of Tarsus, at the far southeastern corner of Asia Minor. This time Darius, King of Kings, was really alarmed. He decided to organize the royal army in order to get rid of Alexander once and for all. He mustered men from all parts of his empire. Innumerable foot soldiers and horsemen from all the various tribes gathered near Babylon. It was difficult to mobilize such a throng, especially since Darius and the upper echelons of his army brought their families along. Each of them had an entourage of servants and slaves, plus carriages stuffed with furniture, silks, and precious jewels. Wherever they halted along the hundreds of miles to the battleground, they pitched luxurious tents decorated with rich carpets. This was hardly the way to wage a war!

For the site of the coming battle, Darius had chosen Issos. But the narrow plain there made it hard for his troops to move, and the Persians were crushed. It was sheer havoc. Panic-stricken, Darius was compelled to watch as his soldiers fell in successive waves. In despair he fled, leaving behind him his own family and heaps of spoils. Alexander behaved kindly to Darius's wife, children, and mother when they were brought to him. He told them that henceforth they must honor him as the master of Asia.

At this point, the Greek army took to the road south along the sea coast and conquered two other important cities. The third city, Tyre, managed to hold out against their attack, for it was built on an island. In the port Alexander constructed a causeway to the island, a road made of stones, gravel, and dirt, enabling his soldiers to attack, while his fleet surrounded Tyre from the sea.

The people of Tyre did their best. They hurled rocks at the soldiers and aimed flaming arrows at the Greek fleet. But there was no way to win, and the siege dragged on and on. From the islands of Rhodes and Cyprus, more ships were added to the Greek fleet. Tyre was unable to hold out any longer and surrendered.

Now Alexander's power was acknowledged by one and all, not only on land but also on the high seas.

After appointing Parmenion, one of his childhood friends, as ruler of the city, Alexander decided to march on to Egypt. It took him and his men seven days to cross the desert. His fleet had arrived and was waiting at the mouth of the Nile. Without even putting up a fight, Memphis—the capital of Egypt—surrendered. The Greeks, and there were many of them in the cities of Egypt, gave Alexander an enthusiastic welcome as their liberator.

Alexander respected the Egyptian gods and ordered sacrifices to them. This made a very favorable impression on the high priests of Egypt, who bestowed on him the title of pharaoh as well as other royal titles. After they had set the regal Egyptian crown on his head, the kingdom of Egypt was considered to have been united with Macedonia.

Alexander intended to build a new city there and give it his name. Before starting out, he decided to visit the famous oracle of Amun and ask where along the Nile the new city should be built.

To reach the oracle he and a few of his companions had to ride deep into a desert. Local guides preceded them and marked the way on the sand. Suddenly the wind began to blow. All the marks that had been left along the way were wiped out. Alexander and his men could see only mounds of sand.

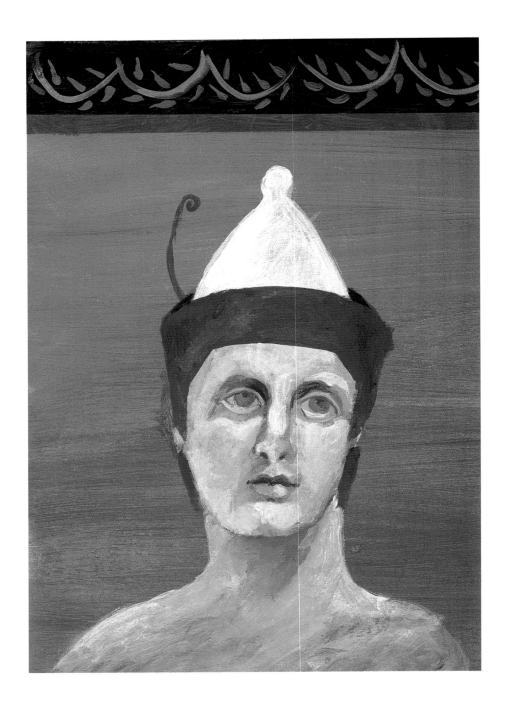

The group had no idea which way to go and became desperate. Just then, two snakes appeared out of the blue. Speaking with human voices, they bade the men follow them. These snakes had been sent by the Egyptian god Amun to show them the way to his temple.

The miracle was interpreted as a sign that the Egyptian god was on Alexander's side. When he finally reached the temple, Amun's prophet told the young king that his fate was to conquer the world. He also showed Alexander precisely where to build the city that would bear his name—Alexandria.

Meanwhile, the Persian king Darius was organizing a new army with soldiers enlisted from all over his empire. There were 200,000 foot soldiers, 45,000 cavalry, 200 chariots, and masses of elephants waiting for the Greeks at Gaugamela. As soon as Alexander heard about all this, he hastened to mobilize his own army.

He built two bridges that crossed first the Euphrates and then the Tigris rivers. One morning his troops found themselves face to face with the Persian army. This was to be the largest-scale battle of all. The Persians were soon annihilated by the skillful movements of the Greeks. And Darius, as usual, fled for his life.

Instead of pursuing him, Alexander and his men headed for Babylon. This beautiful city, full of the riches and palaces of Darius, offered no resistance.

As was his habit, Alexander made sacrifices to the local gods of the city. This had a soothing effect on the people of the city, who then no longer looked upon him as a foreign conqueror.

Alexander entered in triumph. The crowds of men, women, and children showered flower petals on him, and the elders gave him precious gifts. The Persian guardian of the palace treasures handed over the keys.

Alexander appointed two of Darius's administrators to high positions, and his trust in them persuaded them to accept him as their new master.

All roads led to Susa, the actual capital of the Persian empire. Alexander and his men were welcomed as warmly there as in Babylon. Alexander was offered camels and Indian elephants.

Susa was where the great kings of Persia stored their treasures, all of which belonged to Alexander now: mounds of gold, silver, and precious stones. It was at this time that coins with the head of Alexander were minted and circulated widely. There must have been a great many of these coins, because we still find them buried deep in the ground or for sale in antique shops.

Every so often Alexander mobilized more infantry and cavalry from Macedonia, as well as other Greek mercenaries. On the other hand, he sent married or sick soldiers back home. After replenishing his army with vigorous men, he was ready to move on to another great city: Persepolis.

On the way, Alexander and his men were attacked several times by bands of Persians who tried to stop them. This put the soldiers in a nasty mood, and when they entered this city of splendid rich palaces, they started plundering. They killed all the men and made slaves of the women.

Persepolis yielded many more treasures for Alexander. To transport them, he needed 10,000 pairs of mules and 5,000 camels.

The local people disapproved when Alexander went up to the acropolis and to the royal palace, where he sat on the throne as if he were the King of Kings himself.

That same night, after a drunken revel, soldiers were permitted to burn the palace. This was not Alexander's usual way of doing things, and at a later point he tried to make excuses for it. He claimed it was intended as a punishment of the Persians for the disaster their king Xerxes had caused the city of Athens 150 years earlier.

After his defeat at Gaugamela, Darius had gone to Ecbatana, the city far to the east where his summer palace was situated. He was still extremely wealthy and in a position to organize a new army. But when he was told that Alexander was still pursuing him, he retreated yet again with as much of his army and wealth as he could carry. Along the way Darius and his generals had to abandon their supplies and families. Here and there, groups of his soldiers remained behind, waiting and now hoping to save themselves by joining Alexander's army.

Darius's closest companions had lost their confidence in him as a leader, so they decided to murder him. They killed him in his sleep. They imagined that this act would please Alexander, but they were wrong. He punished the murderers and ordered a royal funeral in honor of Darius.

Alexander's aim was to make the Persian elite accept him as the rightful heir to the throne. He needed their cooperation. Many of his Greek soldiers had returned home, while the rest were tired and unwilling to carry on. With Darius's death, they thought they had fulfilled the purpose of their expedition. But not so Alexander. He did not want to go back: there was more of the world to discover and conquer. He longed to move on to the far reaches of Asia.

He summoned his men and spoke to them with great enthusiasm. He was a very persuasive orator, and they agreed to follow him once again.

They set out for what is known today as Afghanistan. But the Greeks, even Alexander's own generals, were worn out, and the disputes increased. His friend Philotas worked up the courage to state in public what all the others were saying in private, although nobody had dared to say it to Alexander's face.

Philotas said that Alexander was acting like a Persian monarch, following the customs of the Persian court, wearing Persian garments and even the crown of the King of Kings. Apparently he preferred the company of the Persian lords and enjoyed listening to their advice. This was stating the obvious, but Alexander became furious and ordered that Philotas be put to death.

Now the soldiers had to climb the Indian side of the Caucasus Mountains, with the city of Baktra as their destination. But during the climb there were enormous difficulties. There wasn't enough food to go around, and the mountain paths were rough, steep, and dangerous.

The Macedonian generals were very worried as they watched
Alexander continue to change more and more before their very
eyes. He had completely abandoned the customs of his motherland
and turned into a Persian despot. Alexander ignored his friends'
anxieties and became absolutely indifferent to their fears.
Out of spite, he married a lovely local princess named Roxane.
Nevertheless, the wedding was celebrated just as in his native land.
According to the customs of Macedonia, the bridegroom meets
the bride with a loaf of bread in his hands and then uses his sword
to cut the bread in half for the couple to share.

He also advised his soldiers to marry local women and to beget children in order not to feel homesick for Greece.

By now his army had thinned out, because in every city he conquered, he had left behind Greek garrisons. He reorganized his men and recruited local soldiers. When the time came to set out for India, he was at the head of an army that was no longer Greek.

Before departing on this new adventure, he tried to find out as much as possible about the people of India. He met local dignitaries and adopted their style of dress, wanting them to consider him one of themselves. He needed their support. He learned as much as he could about the various disputes and conflicts among them in order to decide who his allies should be.

His childhood friends Perdiccas and Hephaistion, accompanied by an Indian prince, were sent with soldiers up to the mountain villages to consolidate Alexander's rule. With the rest of his army, he proceeded to the Indus River Valley lying in the shadow of the Himalaya Mountains.

They met with much resistance, and there were many violent clashes. Battle techniques were different in India, for the various tribes were independent, unlike the tribes under Persian rule. Alexander's men were not used to guerrilla warfare, and he was obliged to form mobile army units and adopt new tactics.

Because of the hardships of such a long journey and so many battles, Alexander and his men had become very hard and cruel. Without the slightest hesitation, they killed thousands of people and plundered and sacked whole cities.

In India, one such sacking took place at Aornos. After a hard battle his victorious soldiers rounded up 230,000 oxen from the area. Alexander chose the largest and healthiest of the oxen and sent them off to Macedonia to plow the fields there.

In India he did as he had done before. Following each victory and before marching on, he left garrisons to watch over each post. But in this area they did not last long. As soon as Alexander was out of sight, the princes of India attacked and killed them.

One of Alexander's main enemies was the Indian king Poros, who rejected the Macedonian's rule as king of India. Poros refused to pay Alexander's taxes and forbade him to cross the boundaries of the kingdom. So Alexander dispatched 6,000 foot soldiers and 5,000 cavalry to Poros's kingdom. In the middle of the night, the invaders crossed the Hydaspes River to confront Poros, thousands of his soldiers, 200 elephants, and 300 horse-drawn chariots.

But Poros's chariots got stuck in the muddy riverbank and were useless. The elephants, however, trampled many Greek foot soldiers to death. King Poros's generals and two sons were killed, and Poros himself was wounded in the savage fighting. He surrendered. Alexander let the Indian king keep his title and kingdom, because he was well aware that he himself did not have enough men to control the newly won land. But Poros gave Alexander 5,000 Indian soldiers and lots of elephants to continue his march down the Indus Valley.

The cities of India fell, in succession, to Alexander's forces and military skill. His aim now was to march east to reach the Ganges River and face the next strong kingdom of India. But his army had reached the end of its endurance. His soldiers were exhausted. Eight long years had gone by since the start of the expedition. The Macedonian men longed to return home, so they rebelled against going farther east.

Up until now, Alexander had been able to convince them to carry on with him. Not any longer. An old soldier stood up and reminded him of all the men who had been killed or had died as a result of sickness and hardships. Many others had been forced to remain in garrisons in distant lands with hardly any hope of ever returning to their homeland. Only 334 men remained with Alexander of the thousands and thousands who had set out from Macedonia eight years before.

Alexander spent that night wide awake in his tent. He needed to reflect and make up his mind what to do. The next day he came out and announced in public that this was the end of the expedition to Asia. He told his soldiers to get ready for the journey back home. Twelve tall altars were built along the banks of the Hyphasis River to mark the end of Alexander's conquests.

On his way back, Alexander halted twice in order to found two more cities. One of them he named Nikaia, from the Greek word for *victory*, and the other Bucephala in honor of his favorite horse, which had died of old age.

In the winter of 325 B.C. he reached Patala, near the mouth of the Indus River. Here, Alexander decided to divide his army into three sections. One section of foot soldiers and elephants would go back the way the army had come, led by Krateros. The second section, under the leadership of Nearchos, was sent by ship along the coast of the Indian Ocean and Persian Gulf. Alexander would lead the third section by a land route close to the seacoast. He hoped to meet his ships in ports along the way and provide them with food and water.

Finally, young Alexander and his men set out on their return trip. They had to cross the vast Baluchistan Desert. Thousands of his men died of hunger and thirst. Only when they reached Pura were they able to rest and recover for a brief interval.

In Carmania Alexander built another city named after himself. He organized sacrifices to the gods as well as games, parades, symposia, and other festivities that lasted seven days.

Then he went on to Persepolis and Susa. There he discovered that the rulers he had appointed had been unjust and corrupt. They had overtaxed the people and kept all the money for themselves. They thought Alexander had been lost in India and would never return to check up on them. But now that he had returned, he punished them severely for their misdeeds.

In Susa, in accordance with Persian custom, he married two princesses, both of whom were descendants of Darius. On the same day, in a special ceremony, many of his officers married Persian girls from important families. Alexander considered these marriages political acts of alliance and guarantees of continuing cooperation between Macedonians and Persians.

His companions disagreed with his actions. They resented his orders to learn the language of foreigners and to dress in clothes they considered odd. They were even more angry about his bestowing Greek military titles on Persians. Soldiers who had been faithful to him up until then perceived the risk that, before long, strangers could replace them entirely in his affections.

But suddenly Alexander told them of his new plan. It was to sail around Arabia, by the Persian Gulf and the Red Sea, to Egypt and the Mediterranean. Then, with Egypt as his base, he would conquer Carthage on the North African coast and Rome in Italy. Apparently there was to be no returning home to Greece for him.

The new campaign was hardly more than a plan forming in his mind when his closest friend, Hephaistion, unexpectedly died in Ecbatana. Alexander went there for the funeral. He was extremely sorrowful, but there was much to be done before the next campaign. He was obliged to welcome foreign dignitaries, who kept pouring in from every corner of the world, to play the role of judge, and to take part in various revels.

On one such occasion in Babylon, after a long bout of drinking, Alexander decided to take a swim in order to sober up. But afterward, he became very ill. His condition grew worse with each passing day, until he was actually burning with fever. Anxiously, his best friends stood near him, hoping against hope that he would get better.

But he realized that he would not. "I leave my kingdom to the best man," he said. Four days later he died.

A splendid chariot was constructed to carry Alexander's body back to his birthplace in Macedonia. But it never took him there.

The fight over who would inherit the lands he had conquered caused one of his closest companions, Ptolemy, to steal Alexander's body. He took it to Egypt and buried it somewhere in Alexandria, his own kingdom. With Alexander's body in his possession, Ptolemy hoped to be considered the rightful heir to the empire.

Sadly, Alexander never returned to his motherland. But he
lived on in the legends and tales of all the peoples he conquered.
He was portrayed in different ways, sometimes as an ancient
Greek, sometimes as a Persian, sometimes as an Indian or
Egyptian. This was precisely how he wanted to be remembered:
constantly changing according to the different civilizations he
came to know as he traveled the world.

Perhaps the most authentic portrayal of Alexander the Great
is as the Ruler of the World crowned with the moon and the sun,
symbol of Vergina.

The End

BLACK SEA

MACEDONIA

Pella

Granikos River

Sardis

Gordion

Ephesos
Miletos

Rhodes

Halikarnassos

Crete

Tarsus

Issos

Gaugamela

Tigris River

Euphrates River

MEDITERRANEAN SEA

Tyre

Damascus

Babylon

Alexandria

Gaza

Amun shrine

Memphis

Nile River

ARABIA

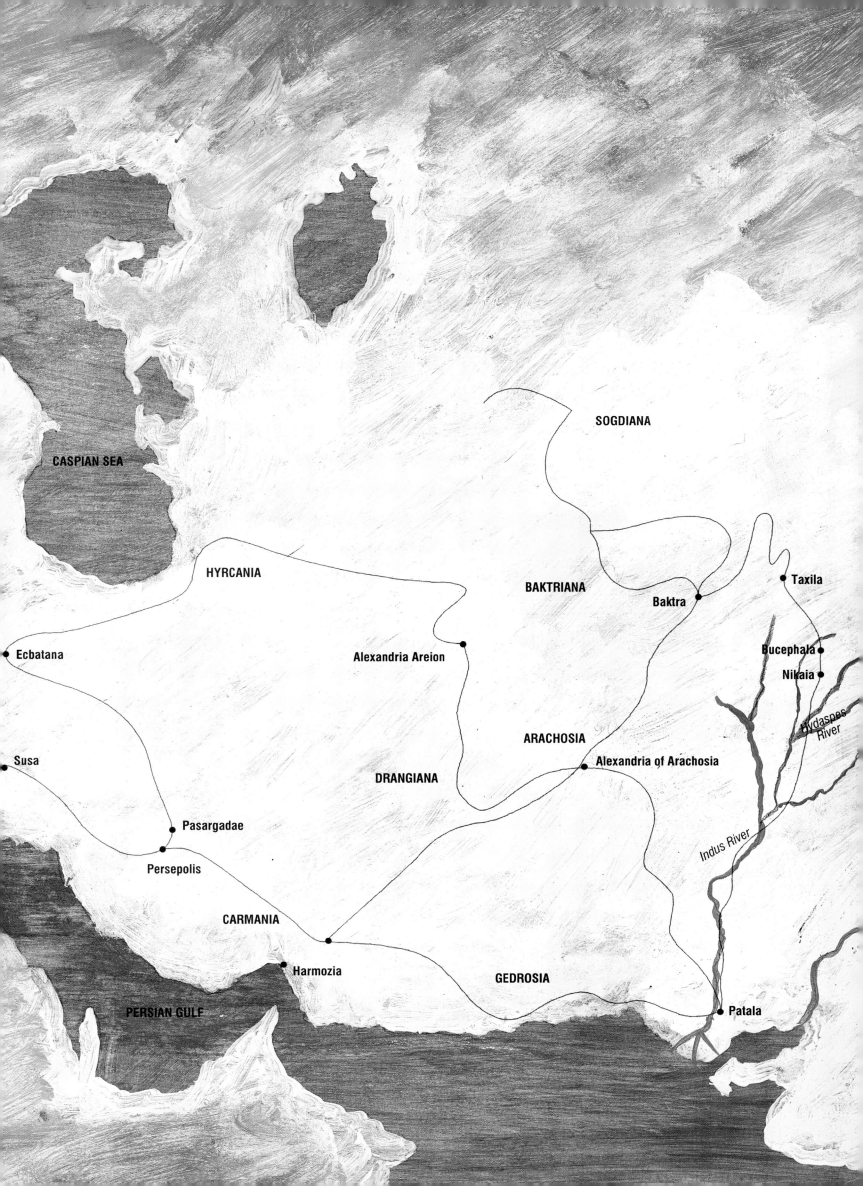

CASPIAN SEA

HYRCANIA

Ecbatana

Susa

Pasargadae

Persepolis

CARMANIA

Harmozia

PERSIAN GULF

SOGDIANA

BAKTRIANA

Baktra

Taxila

Alexandria Areion

Bucephala

Nikaia

Hydaspes River

ARACHOSIA

Alexandria of Arachosia

DRANGIANA

Indus River

GEDROSIA

Patala

© 1993 Kedros Publishers
First published in Greek by Kedros Publishers

English translation © 2004 J. Paul Getty Trust

First published in the
United States of America in 2004 by
Getty Publications
1200 Getty Center Drive, Suite 500
Los Angeles, California 90049-1682
www.getty.edu

Publisher: Christopher Hudson
Editor in Chief: Mark Greenberg

Translator: Alkistis Dimas
Managing Editor: Ann Lucke
Editor: Mollie Holtman
Production Coordinator: Anita Keys
Designer: Jim Drobka

Library of Congress Cataloging-in-Publication Data

Zarabouka, Sofia.
   [Megalexandros. English]
   The story of Alexander the Great / Sofia Zarabouka; translated by
Alkistis Dimas.
      p. cm.
Originally published in Greek in 1993.
ISBN 0-89236-755-5 (hardcover)
1. Alexander, the Great, 356–323 B.C. 2. Greece — History — Macedonian
Expansion, 359–323 B.C. 3. Generals — Greece — Biography. 4.
Greece — Kings and rulers — Biography. I. Title.
DF234.Z37 2004
938'.07'092 – dc22

                          2003023719

Printed and bound in Greece by Kedros Publishers